The Boy Who Didn't Know His Rights

PATRICIA BAILEY

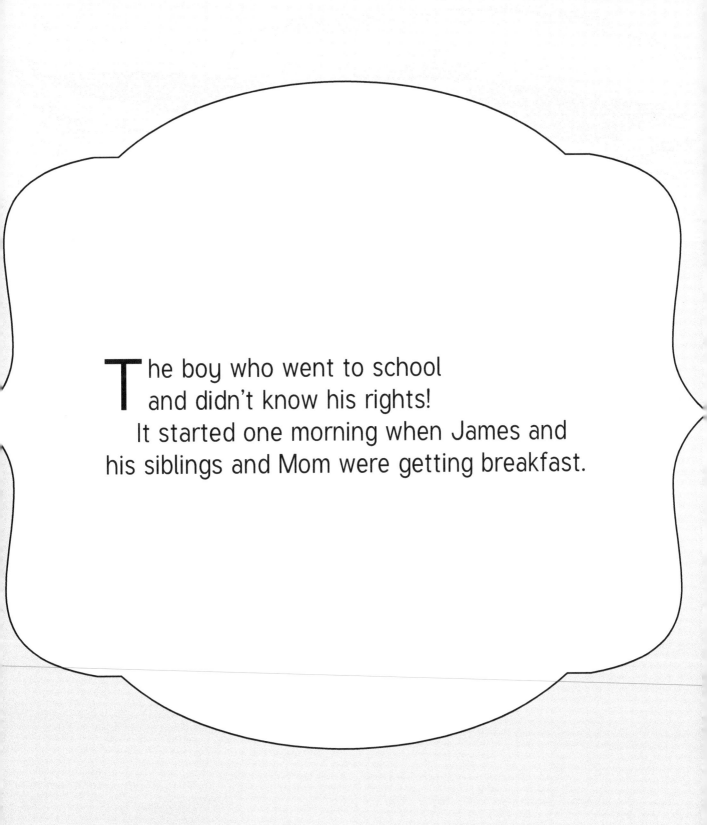

The boy who went to school
and didn't know his rights!
It started one morning when James and
his siblings and Mom were getting breakfast.

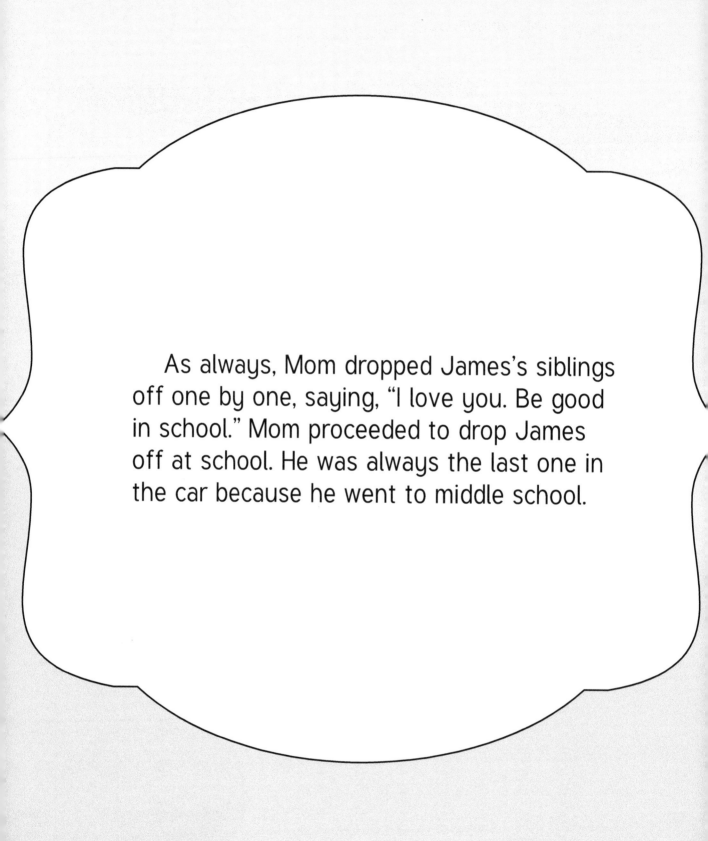

As always, Mom dropped James's siblings off one by one, saying, "I love you. Be good in school." Mom proceeded to drop James off at school. He was always the last one in the car because he went to middle school.

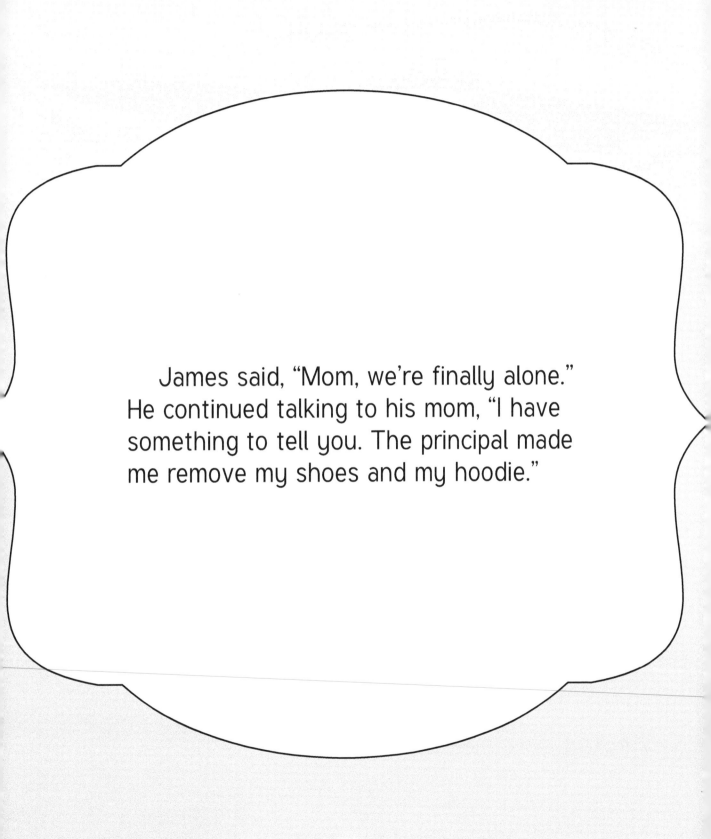

James said, "Mom, we're finally alone." He continued talking to his mom, "I have something to tell you. The principal made me remove my shoes and my hoodie."

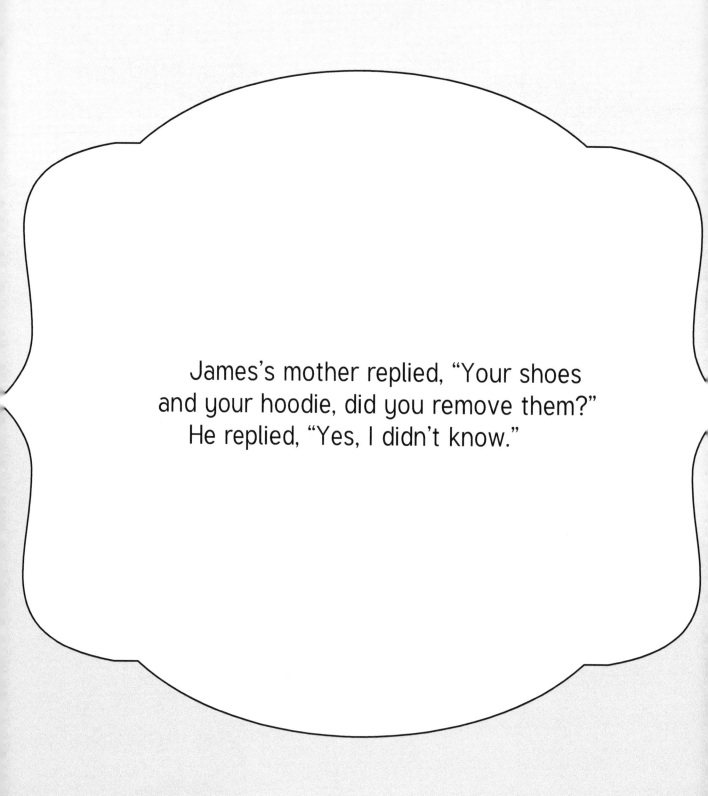

James's mother replied, "Your shoes
and your hoodie, did you remove them?"
He replied, "Yes, I didn't know."

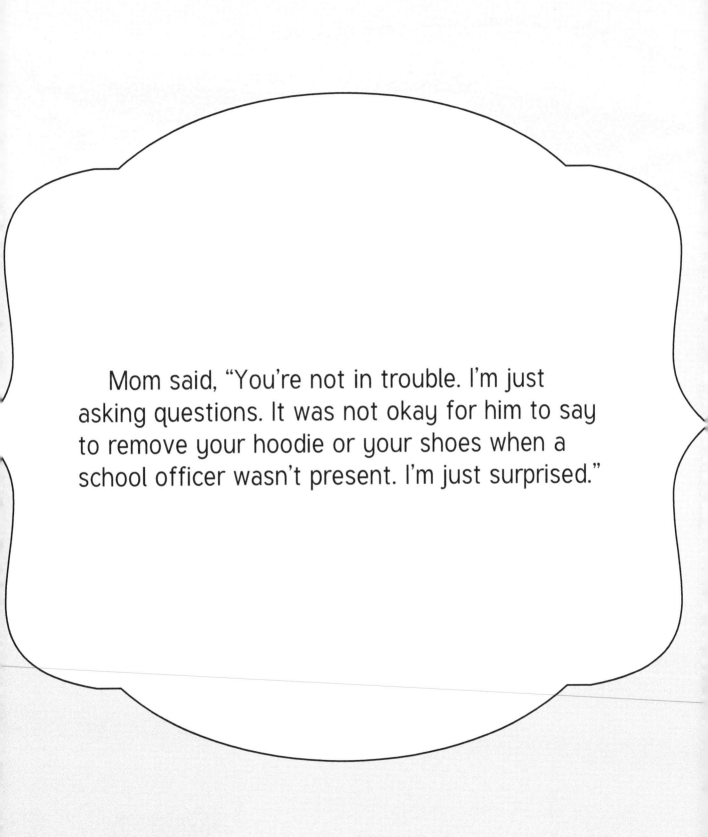

Mom said, "You're not in trouble. I'm just asking questions. It was not okay for him to say to remove your hoodie or your shoes when a school officer wasn't present. I'm just surprised."

James was only eleven years of age, being accused of stealing money by another student that didn't really even have any money in his possession at all. James felt like he was young and actually nervous and didn't even know how to respond to that adult that was accusing him, frisking him in school, away from home without any guardian being present. No one called his mom, not once; not a teacher was there. Anyone as an individual, in school or on the streets, still has rights at an event, on school property, and outside in the community as well.

So all James's mom knew that she has to teach him his Miranda rights and the no frisk law.

"It's time to have a discussion about your rights, so that way, you'll know not to remove any clothing under any circumstances. Learning your Miranda rights, every young man and every woman and every child should know these rights. We can start with the right to remain silent, meaning, that you don't say anything if I'm not present or a lawyer. That's your right as an individual. Do you understand?"

James said, "Yes, Mom."

"James, you also have a right to be warned that anything you say can and will be against you. Meaning, if you say anything, they can hold that against you, so that's why you do not say anything unless I am present or a lawyer or a family member. Do you understand?" His mom quoted once again, "And also, James, you have a right for an attorney. Do you understand?"

He said, "Yes, ma'am, I understand."

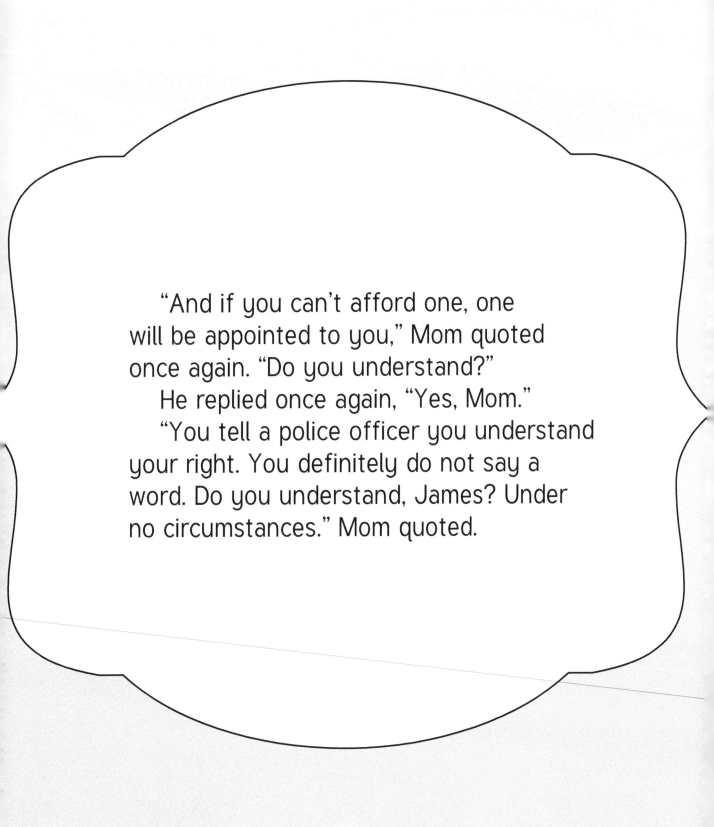

"And if you can't afford one, one will be appointed to you," Mom quoted once again. "Do you understand?"

He replied once again, "Yes, Mom."

"You tell a police officer you understand your right. You definitely do not say a word. Do you understand, James? Under no circumstances." Mom quoted.

"I'm sitting here, letting you know that all lives matter in or out of school. We all have rights. Never forget that, James. There are still more of your rights that you should know. Stop and frisk law. If the police approach and question you, police can lawfully ask you questions if you're in a public place and with an individual. You should ask the officer if you can walk away. If the officer says no, ask why. Do you understand?"

"Yes, Mom. Don't leave. What is a stop?"

"When a police officer acts in a way that you would make a reasonable person feel not free to leave. For example, ordering you to stop or physically hurt you, that is considered as a stop in the fourth amendment. Do you understand, James?" Mom called it once again.

"Yes, Mom."

"And make sure you clarify why you are being stopped, questioned, or arrested. That's your right. Do you understand?" Mom quoted it once again.

"What is a frisk?"

"When police pat or sweep the outside of someone's clothes to check if you have weapons. Are you comprehending everything I'm saying, James? Even without your consent, if they have reasonable suspicion or facts to believe you have a weapon. I know this is a lot to consume in one day, James, but you must know your rights and never wait two weeks to tell me anything do you understand mom replied I love you with all my heart James all of you!!!!!! And don't want anything to happen to you an any kind of way. It's always good to tell your parents firsthand. Don't wait! A situation as serious as this one needs immediate attention."

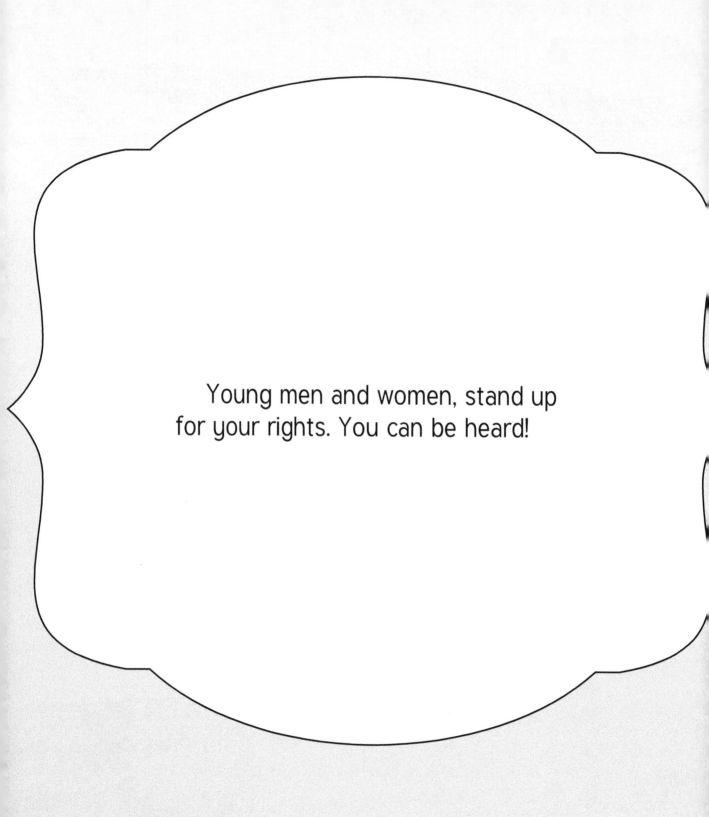

Young men and women, stand up
for your rights. You can be heard!

http://www.mirandarights.org/
https://www.ojp.gov/ncjrs/virtual-library/
abstracts/stop-and-frisk-0

About the Author

Patricia Bailey is a mother of four, with twelve grandchildren that she adores. She is an early childhood educator who loves children of all nations. They are the future, and bringing awareness to young minds will help them in their future along the way.

Lightning Source UK Ltd.
Milton Keynes UK
UKHW051915090223
416667UK00005B/118